Popcorn-Eating SQUIRRELS Go Nuts on Everest

Popcorn-Eating SQUIRRELS Go Nuts on Everest

MATT DICKINSON

ILLUSTRATED BY
CALLOWAY BERKELEY O'REILLY

shrine
bell

www.shrinebell.com

PUBLISHER'S NOTE
No squirrels were harmed in the course of writing this book. Several did, however, get quite cold.

Popcorn-Eating Squirrels Go Nuts on Everest
Matt Dickinson

First published in 2019 by Shrine Bell, an imprint of Vertebrate Publishing.

 Shrine Bell
Omega Court, 352 Cemetery Road, Sheffield S11 8FT, United Kingdom.
www.shrinebell.com

A CIP catalogue record for this book is available from the British Library.

ISBN 978-1-911342-42-7

10 9 8 7 6 5 4 3 2 1

Design and production by Jane Beagley, Vertebrate Publishing.
Illustration colour work by Ewen Kirkpatrick.
www.v-publishing.co.uk

Shrine Bell and Vertebrate Publishing are committed to printing on paper from sustainable sources.

MIX
Paper from responsible sources
FSC
www.fsc.org   FSC® C138821

Printed and bound in Europe by Latitude Press.

FOR
MAGNUS

CHAPTER 1

'I NAME THIS SHIP ...'

It was a helter-skelter journey across town. Four squirrels in a race against time:

BEN

CASSIE

ALFIE

SALTY

Four *hungry* squirrels with one thing on their minds.

POPCORN!

'Get a move on!' Ben cried. 'The boat's about to launch!'

Ben was the route finder. The others followed, jumping from rooftop to rooftop, scampering from tree to tree.

Salty trailed behind, puffing and panting, his tufty ears dripping with sweat.

'Not so fast, pals,' he moaned. 'Your old

pal Salty is running out of steam! My poor wee paws are getting awful sore!'

'Keep up!' Cassie said sternly. 'We're almost there.'

In the distance they could see the glittering outline of the shiny new cruise ship.

The cruise ship with a six-screen cinema on board.

The cruise ship that would be a floating paradise for popcorn-addicted squirrels.

The cruise ship with the biggest popping machine on the PLANET!

'All we have to do is smuggle ourselves on board,' Ben puffed, 'hide away in the cinema and wait for the messy humans to leave us our favourite treat. Day after day.'

'Popcorn of our dreams, yay!' yelled Alfie, the youngest of the squirrels. 'Alfie wants caramel!'

Finally they made it to the docks, climbing into the cabin of a crane where

they could spy on the scene.

'Wow!' Alfie gasped. 'It's the bestest ship in the whole wiggly world.'

The squirrels gaped at the sleek lines of the huge cruise ship, fresh paint gleaming brilliantly, the rows of cabins stretching as high as a skyscraper, the scarlet funnels splendid in the early morning sun.

The *Esmerelda Exotica*. The height of luxury, flagship of the Esmerelda fleet.

Cassie frowned, her shiny nose wrinkling. 'There's something odd about this. Where are the passengers? Why isn't the party starting?'

'It's true,' Ben said. 'There's something wrong.'

The squirrels stared at the strangely quiet dockside.

Only a handful of people were there, the Lord Mayor among them, decked in chains of glittering gold. He was cracking his knuckles, glancing frequently at his watch. Strings of gaily coloured bunting fluttered mockingly above his head. Next to him was a journalist with a camera. From time to time she yawned and scratched her neck.

A brass band was standing nearby, shuffling their feet and unsure what to do, their trumpets and trombones glimmering in the sunlight but silent as the grave.

Food stall chefs were busy cooking, but no one was buying the treats. Because no one was there.

It was a once-in-a-lifetime event to celebrate the maiden voyage of a brand new cruise ship. And hardly a soul had turned up. Hardly a soul but four hungry squirrels and the distinguished-looking gentleman who was climbing out of a silver Rolls-Royce car at that very moment – the owner of the vessel, Sir Archibald Kevino Rapscallion Buck.

CHAPTER 2

PARTY POOPERS

'My dear S-S-S-Sir Archibald,' the mayor stuttered as he approached the vehicle, 'I can only apologise for the—'

'Out of my way, you clown,' Sir Archibald snapped.

He prodded the mayor in the chest with his silver-tipped cane, smoothing back his greying locks with a hand that glimmered with gem-laden rings.

'I'm ruined,' he cried. 'Ruined, I tell you! I've spent millions on this boat and not a single passenger has turned up.'

The mayor nodded, his face a picture of grim misery.

'The town's been down on its luck,' he said. 'The people haven't got a lot of spare cash for luxury holidays.'

'The *Exotica* is a wonder,' Sir Archibald continued. 'Why can't they see that? Four swimming pools, a shopping arcade, a six-screen cinema with its very own Pop-O-Matic 3000 – the most advanced popcorn-making machine in the universe. It's irresistible!'

Up in the cabin of the crane, Alfie breathed in deeply, closing his eyes dreamily as an unmistakeable aroma drifted across from the ship.

'Alfie smells the sweetness,' he said in awe. 'The best smell in the whole wide world.'

Alfie's friends sniffed at the air, their moist little noses trembling.

'Popcorn!' Salty muttered, drool running down the side of his mouth.

'Caramel. Butterscotch. Salty. Plain,' Ben whispered. 'Popcorn is the nectar of the gods!'

Nearby they heard a vehicle backfire. A rickety old van pulled into the docks.

'I think there are some passengers after all,' Ben nodded towards the van.

The decrepit old banger pulled up next to the mayor and Sir Archibald. Dark blue smoke spewed out of the exhaust as the engine rattled and died.

Painted shakily on the side of the van the squirrels read the following:

EVEREST OR BUST
POPPING ALL THE WAY
TO BASE CAMP

The doors of the van crashed open and two characters – a man and a woman – jumped out.

'Oh no!' Cassie exclaimed, her ears folding back.

Salty gasped. Alfie gulped. Ben just stared, his eyes wide as saucers.

An elderly woman in a faded ballgown. An orange-tanned man in a cheap and nasty grey suit.

'Rosalba and Fandango,' Cassie whispered, her voice dripping with dread.

It was true. Two enemies of the squirrels from an epic battle that had been fought not long ago. A battle that had seen a cinema destroyed. A battle that had seen popcorn falling from the skies across the entire land. A battle in which our friends

had survived only by becoming temporary squirrel superheroes.

'I hope we're not too late for the sailing,' Rosalba trilled. 'We need a lift to Mumbai. We're on our way to Everest Base Camp.'

'You don't look like climbing types … ' Sir Archibald said with a suspicious frown. 'What's the big idea?'

Rosalba gave Sir Archibald her sweetest look, her false eyelashes fluttering like tango-dancing spiders.

'Just a few hours ago I was cast adrift on the seven seas,' she cried, 'condemned by a cruel crew of evil squirrels to a watery grave. Only by the strangest twists of fate did my saviour—'

'Evil squirrels?' Sir Archibald snapped impatiently. 'What the blazes are you talking about, woman?'

'I know,' Rosalba said, 'it doesn't sound terribly likely, does it? But it's true, I tell you!'

She patted aggressively at her nose with a powder puff for a few seconds, then continued.

'Anyway, Fandango here was a total *star*! He hired a boat and came out to rescue me and my associates.'

'I recognise you,' Sir Archibald said, staring at Fandango. 'You're the inventor of the Pop-O-Matic 3000, aren't you? The one we've got on board?'

Fandango took a bow. 'I am indeed,' he muttered, ' … not that I like to mention it.'

'As a thank you for saving my life, I promised Fandango I would make his most cherished wish come true,' Rosalba continued.

The bored journalist stepped forward, her interest spiked. She pulled out her notepad and pencil.

'What is the wish?' she asked.

Up in the cabin, the squirrels leaned forward, their ears pricked up.

CHAPTER 3

POPTASTIC PROPOSALS

'To cook popcorn at Everest Base Camp!'
Fandango said. 'It was my father's dream
and now it's mine!'

'What an amazing idea!' the journalist
exclaimed, scribbling rapidly in her
notepad. 'Do tell me more.'

'My father was a master popcorn maker,'
Fandango said proudly. 'And he also
loved to climb. All his life he wanted to
pop corn in the shadow of the highest
mountain on earth, but he passed away
before he could do it. In his honour I will
try to complete the quest!'

'What a great story!' the journalist said.
'Can I get a picture?'

Rosalba and Fandango gave a cheesy
smile for the camera as Sir Archibald

stepped forward to get in the shot.

'You know what? You're on to something there!' Sir Archibald said. 'It's a fantastic publicity-grabbing idea. The press will go crazy for it! But why stop at Base Camp?'

He paused dramatically, then added, 'Why not pop corn at the top of the world?'

Up in the crane, the squirrels shivered with excitement.

'Popcorn on the summit of Everest!' Alfie gasped.

'It's a bonny wee plan,' Salty whispered, rubbing his paws together in deep thought.

Down on the dock, Sir Archibald seemed in the grip of a bizarre fever. He strutted back and forth like a crazy chicken, arms waggling in the air.

'This is the answer! Don't you all see?' he hissed, his eyeballs rolling wildly. 'This idea can save my whole business! You –

can you shoot video on that camera?'

'Sure,' the journalist replied, pressing a switch.

'I hereby announce a challenge!' Sir Archibald declared, staring manically into the lens. 'A challenge unlike any the world has ever seen. A challenge that will captivate the entire universe in its boldness and daring—'

'Get on with it,' the journalist muttered.

'I, Sir Archibald Kevino Rapscallion Buck, do hereby announce I will award *a million pounds* and provide popcorn *for life* to the first team to cook popcorn on the summit of Mount Everest! All you have to do is book a passage on my new vessel, the *Esmerelda Exotica*, and you will be transported to the port of Mumbai in India where the road journey into the Himalayan mountains will begin! The ship sails at sunset! Make haste to the docks!'

High in the cabin of the crane, four

totally stunned squirrels turned to stare at each other.

For a few seconds they were frozen to the spot. Alfie was the first to move, jiggling from foot to foot like a tap dancer.

'D-d-d-did he say … popcorn … for *life?*' the smallest squirrel squeaked. 'For life! For life!'

He started to run around the cabin at high speed, his eyeballs swivelling in opposite directions.

Salty grabbed hold of Alfie, spinning him round and round in a dance of joy.

'A million pounds! Oh, my heart is fair set to explode with happiness, so it is, pals! We'll be laughing all the way to the bank!'

Ben and Cassie were still motionless. Ben looked at Cassie. Their expressions shared none of the joy and excitement of their friends. She nodded back at him.

'Not so fast,' Ben exclaimed. 'There's no way we're going to Everest, my friends.

It's far too dangerous for the likes of us.'

Alfie wasn't listening.

'Alfie gets popcorn for life!' he sang. 'Climb a silly little mountain and it's ours! Ours! All ours!'

'*Silly little mountain*?!' Cassie said, her voice squeakier than usual. 'We're talking cruel crevasses, awful avalanches, scary storms. Squirrels do not belong there! End of story.'

'Cassie's right,' Ben said. 'We'd be up against professional climbers and explorers. They know what they're doing and we don't.'

The four squirrels argued the points back and forth for more than an hour as Ben and Cassie tried to reason with their friends.

Finally Salty turned to Ben, his lips fixed in a petulant pout.

'Well, I'm going to Everest whatever you say!' he uttered. 'You think Salty the squirrel is scared of a wee bit of fluffy snow, do you? I've climbed more mountains than you've eaten acorns, pal, so mind out of my way!'

'Alfie coming with you!' Alfie cried.

Before Ben and Cassie could act, the two squirrels were out of the cabin and shimmying down the ladder to the ground.

CHAPTER 4

VIRAL ARRIVALS

Alfie and Salty gasped. The scene on the dockside had changed completely. Sir Archibald Buck's Everest popcorn challenge had instantly gone viral and the place was now buzzing with the excited chatter of thousands.

The two squirrels pushed their way through the crowd.

'Stick with me, pal,' Salty said. 'I'll keep you safe, my wee friend.'

Sir Archibald had erected a platform so he could be seen above the crowd. He bellowed across them with a megaphone.

'Book yourself a cabin!' he cried. 'There aren't many left , so look sharp! Think of it: a million pounds and popcorn for life! Roll up! Roll up!'

The brass band struck up a rousing tune. The food stalls were doing a roaring trade, the air rich with the smell of hotdogs and onions, candyfloss and toffee apples.

Men, women and children from all over the land were shuffling up the gangplank of the mighty cruise ship, laden down with rucksacks and ropes and expedition supplies.

The two squirrels were struggling to make progress through the dense crowd when the journalist appeared in front of them, her camera ready.

'I'm Alice Snapworthy from the *Blackwater Bugle*,' she said, her face glowing with a lovely wide smile as she bent down to squirrel height. 'I'm doing a feature on the animal teams that have accepted the challenge. Can we have a chat?'

'*Other* animal teams?' Salty said, his nose wrinkling like he'd just sniffed a rotten acorn. 'What *type* of other animal teams? I thought we were the only ones.'

'Well there's him, for example.' The journalist pointed to a sinister-looking character nearby.

'It's a mole!' Alfie said excitedly. 'Alfie *loves* moles – they're all diggy and daggy and … *moley*!'

The tiny mole really was a bizarre sight, not least because he was wearing

a massive rucksack and carrying an ice axe. Not something you see on a mole every day of the week. Half the size of the squirrels, his jet-black fur gleamed in the early morning sun, his huge, shovel-like hands by his side.

The curious-looking beast turned his head slowly and stared at them through the bottle-bottom lenses of his extra-strength glasses.

The sun passed behind a cloud, casting a strange chill in the air. Alfie shivered.

'That,' said the journalist, her smile freezing just a touch, 'is Wilberforce, the high-altitude mole.'

The small mole strolled casually towards them. He looked the two squirrels up and down.

'Don't go to Everest, old chaps,' he said finally, his posh accent ringing clear. 'You'll *die*.'

Salty's fur bristled.

'Die? DIE? Salty the squirrel is forged

out of solid iron girders and tungsten nuggets, pal. I'm former SAS special forces, so stick that in your underground tunnel, you sad velvet-furred little worm-muncher!'

'You had better watch your step, old thing,' the mole said quietly, still staring at them. His huge paws twitched a bit by his sides.

'Anyhow, what did you say your name is?' Salty scoffed. '*Wilberforce, the high-altitude mole?* Pish! What kind of a cock-a-doodle name is that, pal?'

The tiny mole looked up at Salty, his spookily milky eyes fixing Salty with a very hard glare.

'It's not just a nickname, dear fellow,' he said, quietly. 'It's who I am. End of story.' He shrugged off his massive rucksack and flexed his surprisingly muscular shoulders. 'You got a problem with that, old bean?'

'Aye, well, it's a wee bit of a stupid name,' Salty said with a snigger.

'Ridiculous, as a matter of fact.'

He winked at the journalist, but she didn't smile back.

Wilberforce took off his glasses. He calmly pulled out a handkerchief and began to polish them.

'No more ridiculous,' he said, 'than if you were called "Salty, the bad-tempered, irritating, fibbing, shouty squirrel".'

All was silent for a second or two. Then the journalist made a strange noise. Almost like a giggle that was strangled into a cough.

Up in the cabin of the crane, Cassie and Ben looked at each other, laughter in their eyes.

'I'm not sure this is going to end well,' Cassie whispered.

Salty was still for a moment. His eyes bulged, and his ears began to twitch. He started pacing rapidly back and forth, his hairy paws slapping hard against the concrete.

CHAPTER 5

DON'T MESS WITH THE MOLE

'Bad-tempered?' Salty snorted. '*Bad-tempered?*' he snarled.

'And rather rudely shouty,' the little mole added.

'Shouty? SHOUTY?' Salty yelled.

'And a jolly old fibber as well,' Wilberforce added, still polishing his glasses.

'I'm no fibber, you dirt-digging doofus!'

'Are!'

'NOT!'

'Are!'

'NOT!'

Salty moved in close to the feisty mole. Close enough their noses were touching.

'All reet, pal, if you think I'm a fibber, why don't you prove it?'

'Okay, I will,' Wilberforce smirked. 'You say you were in the SAS?'

Salty's lower lip wobbled for a moment.

'Aye?' he said. There was an unmistakeable tremor in his voice.

'Well, I was born and raised as a young mole on the parade grounds inside the Special Air Service headquarters in Hereford and I've never seen or heard of you … *pal*.'

'Aye,' Salty blustered, 'but of course I'm talking about the *other* SAS.'

Wilberforce grinned, an entirely empty smile.

'There *is* no other SAS, old bean,' he said.

'Aye, well, that's where you're dead wrong,' Salty barked. 'Coz I'm talking about the er, umm, the Squirrel Attack Squadron.'

'Woweee,' Alfie whistled in admiration, 'the Squirrel Attack Squadron! You're the toughest squirrel ever, Salty!'

Wilberforce threw back his head and laughed out loud.

'Squirrel Attack Squadron?' he snorted. 'Very well: name a single battle that you've fought in.'

'I was at the battle of … of Weasel Ridge, I was, pal,' Salty declared, 'nibbling through the enemy lines with my extra-sharp nibbly teeth!'

'The battle of *Weasel Ridge*?!' Alfie yelled. 'Awesome! You're my hero, Salty!'

'The battle of Weasel Ridge?' the little mole scoffed. 'You'll be telling me next you had a machine gun loaded with acorns?'

Salty jutted out his chest.

'Aye, well, it just so happens I did, pal – a nice shiny gun it was too. A thousand acorns a minute it could fire, and let me tell you: once I had those weasels in my sight, I showed no mercy! They called me the "Weasel Whacker", they did! No mercy at all with a rat-a-tat-a-tat-a—'

'Excuse me!' the journalist interjected, a stern frown across her face. 'This is all very well, but I need my photo before the ship sails. Now, where's the other animal team?'

'Over here!' came a growl.

Pushing through the crowd came the very *last* creatures that Salty and Alfie wanted to see.

'Uh oh!' Alfie exclaimed. He put his tail in his mouth and began to suck it.

Salty's eyes widened. A strange tremor ran through him.

Three powerful-looking critters, black-furred with a bright white stripe down their backs, their eyes as hard as flint, their physique every bit as toned as the most dedicated weightlifter.

Gritsky. Fleabilly. Spudbasher.

The honey badger brothers. The squirrels' most deadly foes.

CHAPTER 6

BADGER OBLIVION

'Well, well, well,' said Gritsky, the chief honey badger, with a sneer. 'If it isn't two of our old friends: the "Popcorn-Eating Squirrels". Not looking quite so superhero now, are you?'

Wilberforce the mole looked confused.

'Last time we saw these idiots they were bundling us into barrels and sending us off to sea,' Gritsky explained. 'It was only thanks to a passing ship that we got rescued.'

'Now we're going to show you who's boss,' Fleabilly added. 'We'll beat you to the summit of Everest, blast off a helping of popcorn, and *we'll* get the million pounds and popcorn for life!'

'You don't need to worry about the

squirrels,' Wilberforce said. 'They're not coming anyway – I got the last ticket.'

Everything went quiet for a few seconds. Salty's left eye began to twitch.

'Did you say you got the ... last ticket?' he said softly.

Alfie sniffed, gulping back a sob.

Wilberforce nodded, pleased with himself. 'Yep.'

'The LAST TICKET?' Salty roared.

Spudbasher stuck out his tongue and blew a raspberry.

'So you pesky squirrels can't go anyway. Ha ha!'

The honey badger brothers broke into an eerie, high-pitched cackle as Salty danced a jig of rage about the dock.

'Alfie won't go to Everest,' wailed Alfie. 'Alfie gutted! Alfie VERY sad.'

Gritsky's face split into an evil grin.

'Never mind, little squirrel,' he said, his voice as sweet as treacle. 'Uncle Gritsky might be able to help you ... '

Alfie blinked, a frown crinkling his brow.

'I've got an idea,' Gritsky hissed to his mates. 'How about we take a mascot with us to the big E?'

'Yeah!' Fleabilly growled. 'We need all the luck we can get.'

He grabbed hold of Alfie, snatching him by the arm.

'No! Wait—' Alfie squeaked.

'Shut up!' snapped Fleabilly.

'All aboard!' came a cry from the podium. Sir Archibald was preparing to close the gangway to the vessel. 'Remaining passengers must board now!'

The honey badger brothers rushed for the gangway, Alfie still gripped in Fleabilly's paws, his eyes wide. Wilberforce was trotting right behind.

Salty raced to help, but he was just too slow to catch up.

Alfie wriggled, trying to slip free.

'Save me, Salty! Save Alfie!' the tiny squirrel called. But he was held in a vice-like grip.

Alfie disappeared from view into the ship just as two security guards barred the gangplank in front of Salty and began to pull it back.

'That's it,' the security man said. 'Those were the last passengers. Bad luck.'

Cassie and Ben raced up at that exact moment. They were moving so fast they almost skidded into the water of the dock.

'What's happened?' Ben looked around frantically.

'It's Alfie,' Salty cried. 'The wee bairn's been kidnapped!'

CHAPTER 7

SWING
TIME

The ship's horn blasted.

PAAAAAAAAAARP!

The squirrels jumped back. Cheers came from the deck. Dockworkers began to loosen the ropes.

'We've got to get on board somehow!' Cassie hissed.

The squirrels looked for a rope they could climb, but the workers were everywhere and the boat was already pulling away.

'I've got an idea,' Ben cried. 'Follow me!'

He led the way back to the crane, scampering up the ladder to the highest point and edging out on to the massive arm.

Cassie followed on right behind him. Salty was at the back as usual, puffing away.

Ahead of them the massive chain was dangling.

'I get it!' Cassie said. 'We use the chain like a swing, yes?'

'Exactly,' Ben said. 'We swing ourselves on board.'

'Quickly!' Cassie said.

The three squirrels shimmied down the metal chain, using the huge steel links as steps. At the end was an enormous hook.

'There's no time to lose!' shouted Ben. 'Swing!'

The squirrels clung together on the hook, shifting their weight, just like children on a playground swing. The mighty chain began to stir.

'Now this way!' Cassie called. 'Now that! Salty, move in the same direction as me and Ben!'

'I'm doing ma best,' Salty huffed.

Below them was the ship, preparing to leave. A great plume of black smoke burped from the funnel. The ropes were all cast away.

The chain swung wider.

'Aim for the pool,' Ben said. Cassie and Salty saw what he meant; the on-board swimming pool would make a perfect splashdown.

PAAAAAAAAAAAARP! went the siren once more. The crowds on the dock cheered and clapped. The brass band played as loudly as they could.

The squirrels strained as they threw their weight back and forth.

The propellers began to spin, swishing the water of the dock into a mini whirlpool. The roar of the crowd filled the air.

The chain was swinging faster, the arc bigger each time.

'One more go!' Cassie screamed. 'Almost ready to launch!'

The mighty ship inched away from the dock.

'One, two, three … ' Ben yelled.

At the crucial moment, Ben and Cassie let go. They zoomed through the air as if they had been shot from a catapult.

Higher and higher, and then down, down, and into the swimming pool they went with a satisfying **SPLASH**.

The two squirrels bobbed up in a spray of water, giving each other a sloshy high five.

'We made it!' Cassie grinned. 'But where's Salty?'

They looked back at the crane. There was Salty, still swinging back and forth.

'Don't be a chicken!' Ben shouted, treading water. 'Go for it before it's too late!'

The *Esmerelda Exotica* was pulling away even further from the dock.

'Are you saying Salty is frit?' Salty yelled back, faintly. 'Are you saying Salty is a scaredy-cat?'

'Just shut up and do it!' Cassie yelled,
rolling her eyes.

Salty swung backwards on the chain and
made his final swing.

At the highest point of the arc he did,
finally, let go.

He zoomed upwards.

'Yay!' Ben cried. 'Good for you, Salty!'

'You see?' Salty called as he whistled
through the air at great velocity, his fur
rippling in the whizzing air, paws clasped
casually behind his head, his legs crossed
in a super-relaxed pose. 'They don't
call Salty the hero of Weasel Ridge for
nothing!'

Two seconds later, Saltworthy McTavish
Finnbar McNutt, legs flailing, eyes
popping wide with the fearful realisation
that everything might not be going *totally*
to plan, did indeed make it on board the
ship.

'Ah ... ' said Ben, grimly.

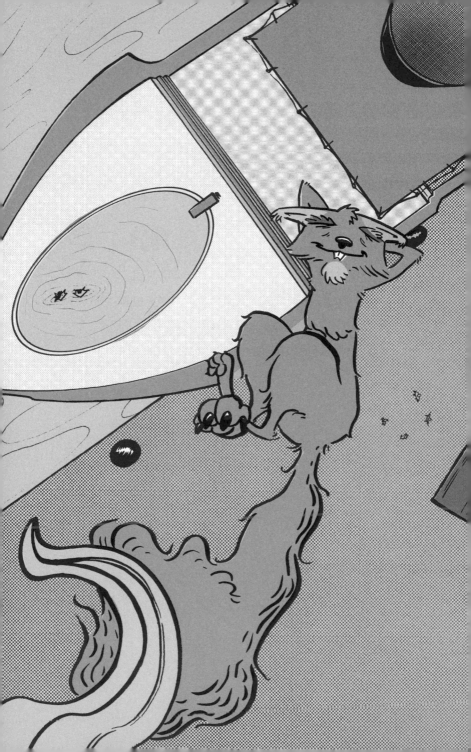

'Hmmmmm … ' said Cassie.

Salty had landed all right. That was the good news.

The bad news was *where* he had landed.

Straight into the funnel of the *Esmerelda Exotica*.

Thirty seconds later a huge **BURP** of oily black smoke spewed from the funnel. The shrieking sound of splintering metal filled the air.

The vessel juddered … and came to a halt.

CHAPTER 8

FUNNEL FURY

'You blithering *nincompoop*! You blundering *disaster*! You engine-wrecking, ship-murdering, funnel-intruding furry *nightmare*!'

Sir Archibald was outraged. The entire ship had to be evacuated. The *Esmerelda Exotica* was steered back in to the dock.

Salty stood before them, dripping with gear oil and smothered head-to-toe in dark soot. A couple of sticking plasters covered his wounds.

Ben and Cassie were back in the cabin of the crane, looking down on the scene as Sir Archibald Buck vented his rage. Alfie was still a prisoner of the honey badger brothers, who were standing nearby in the angry crowd.

'You've ruined everything!' Sir
Archibald screamed. 'Everything!'
  He pointed to the *Esmerelda Exotica*,
tied up once more at the dock, a sad
trickle of smoke creeping from the funnel.
  The crowd of thousands glared at Salty,
hatred blazing from their eyes.
  'That's right, pal,' Salty said bitterly,
'blame me, why don't you? It's always old
Salty's fault, *isn't* it?'

A dark red flush ran across Sir Archibald's face.

'What are you talking about, you ridiculous squirrel? Of course it's your fault! Look at the engineer's report, for goodness sake!'

He slapped a pile of papers in his hand, reading aloud.

'"Cause of engine failure: big fat stupid squirrel gumming up the works!" Could that be any clearer?'

'Fat?' Salty raged. He started strutting backwards and forwards on the dockside. 'Who are you calling fat, pal? Salty *fat*? I'm generously proportioned, and it's all muscle, pal, MUSCLE!'

Salty snatched Sir Archibald's wooden walking stick from him and tried to snap it over his knee. But the stout, hickory-wood cane wasn't about to budge, and Salty hopped across the dock as the pain raged.

'Ow, ow, ow! See what you've done now?' Salty snarled.

Sir Archibald grabbed back his stick. 'Enough!' he yelled. 'Now what do you suggest I do about my broken ship?'

'Ah, nae problem,' Salty said with a shrug. 'Just claim the money back on your insurance.'

Sir Archibald bent down low, so that his bulbous red nose was almost touching Salty's.

'Do you think I'm insured against … ' he growled, consulting the papers again, ' … *squirrel poo* in the engines?'

Alfie's voice suddenly rang out from somewhere in the crowd.

'Yay! Salty did a poo in the engine! Salty pooed in the engine! HA HA!'

Salty's eyes bulged. His tail twitched at high velocity back and forth.

'I've never been so insulted in my *life*,' he raged. 'That must have been some *other* squirrel did that, pal, cos on my poor old wee mum's life it wasn't me, I swear!'

'Was!' snarled Sir Archibald.

'Wasn't!'

'Was!'

WASN'T!'

'Stop it at once!' A bony figure in a faded ballgown stepped from the crowd.

Rosalba! Her rhinestone earrings dangling from her ears, her moth-eaten fur cape draped around her skinny shoulders.

'We're not interested in this baloney!' she cried. 'We want to know what's happening about the Everest popcorn challenge and the million pounds.'

Sir Archibald coughed. He stared down at his shoes.

'You've told the entire world on TV you're going to do it,' Rosalba hissed in his ear. 'Imagine how it will look if you back out now.'

Sir Archibald locked his mouth into a position that looked almost like a smile.

The crowd muttered excitedly.

The photographers clustered in close.

'The challenge is still on!' he proclaimed through gritted teeth. The photographers snapped picture after picture.

'But I'll restrict it to five teams,' he continued quickly, 'and fly you out in my private jet. Five teams only! It's first come, first served!'

The crowd surged forward with a great cry.

Rosalba was in prime position so she got the first of the five places. The honey badger brothers used their superior muscle power to barge through, trampling children and adults underfoot, so they also won a slot on the plane. The press photographers snapped happily away – what a story!

After fifteen minutes the finalists were announced …

- ROSALBA AND FANDANGO.
  Team name: 'Pop to the Top.'
- THE WILMINGTON LADIES
  KNITTING CIRCLE.
  Team name: 'To Knit, or Not to Knit.'
- THE HONEY BADGER BROTHERS.
  Team name: 'Not So Sweet.'
- THE WATLING STREET ROMAN
  RE-ENACTMENT SOCIETY.
  Team name: 'Legion of the Damned.'
- WILBERFORCE THE HIGH-
  ALTITUDE MOLE.
  Team name: 'I'll win, old chap, I'll win.'

Later that day the five teams and all their
popcorn-making machines were loaded
into Sir Archibald's private jet, with Alfie
still being held hostage as the honey
badgers' mascot.

What none of them knew about was the
secret baggage.

Among all the fuss and kerfuffle, Cassie,
Ben and Salty had managed to stow

themselves away on board, hiding inside a Pop-O-Matic 3000.

'We'll rescue Alfie if it's the last thing we do,' Cassie whispered to the others as the aeroplane engines started up with a roar.

The squirrels were off to Everest, the highest mountain on earth. The great adventure had begun!

CHAPTER 9

KATHMANDU CAPERS

At dawn the next day the aeroplane touched down in Kathmandu, the capital of Nepal. The Pop-O-Matic the squirrels were hiding in was unloaded, giving the stowaways their first secret peek at Asia.

Cassie used her paw to wipe moisture off the glass.

'Look at the mountains!' she gasped.

The view was stupendous. The entire northern horizon was filled with awesome, jagged, frozen peaks. They looked like the sharpened fangs of some phantasmagorical, gigantic yeti.

'The Himalaya,' Ben whispered, awestruck. 'Mightiest mountain range on the planet.'

Salty sniffed. 'Call those mountains,

do you? I've seen a lot bigger in Scotland, pal, I can tell you – and that's just from the window of my granny's flat in Glasgow!'

The teams and their gear were taken on a crazy journey through the exotic city. The traffic was mad: cars, trucks, bikes and even cattle, zigzagging crazily to and fro, horns blaring and tooting. The squirrels found their noses twitching with unfamiliar smells: persimmons and cantaloupes on the fruit stalls; the enticing spicy tang of cooking curry drifting from an open window.

From time to time they passed street-food vendors, the air zapping with the sharp sizzle of boiling oil as they fried momos and samosas.

Finally the convoy reached a local square where the expeditions were preparing to set out for Base Camp. There, in the shadow of a mighty temple, climbers and porters were rushing about excitedly, and hundreds of boxes of food and climbing equipment were piled high.

'*Shhhh*!' Cassie cautioned. 'There's Rosalba.'

The squirrels sneaked a look out of the window of the Pop-O-Matic and watched as Rosalba tottered about, blinking in the morning sun.

'Where's my transport?' she demanded, scanning the busy scene with a sour look. 'You surely don't expect me to walk in *these*?'

She pointed a finger at her six-inch-tall stiletto heels.

'This is a serious expedition, my dear,' Sir Archibald told her sharply, 'not a five-star holiday.'

He gestured to the distant mountains, the glittering array of dangerous-looking peaks that seemed to touch the sky.

'That's where we're going,' he snarled. 'Just in case you were in any doubt.'

'Hmmph!' Rosalba replied, stamping

her foot. 'I want a VIP limousine, *immediately.*'

'Me too!' Fandango snapped.

Sir Archibald grinned mysteriously, his lips twitching a little.

'How about a turbocharged *pachyderm*, my sweet friends? Leather and ivory trimmings?'

'Well, I've never heard of that brand of vehicle,' Rosalba sniffed, examining a chip in a gold-lacquered fingernail, 'but it *sounds* quite luxurious.'

'Oh, it is,' Sir Archibald murmured, 'and quite environmentally friendly. It's *dumbo-tronic.*'

Inside their secret hideaway, Salty's left eyebrow shot up approvingly. '*Dumbo-tronic?* That sounds more like it.'

Cassie and Ben had to stuff their paws against their mouths to stop themselves sniggering.

'Yep. Runs on banana leaves,' said Cassie, her eyes glinting mischievously.

Rosalba and Fandango almost fainted when the grumpy old elephant was brought round the corner.

'You're not getting ME on that scabby beast!' Rosalba snorted.

'It's that or walk,' Sir Archibald shrugged.

A few minutes later the two of them were strapped side by side to the top of the reluctant creature.

They all lined up in the dusty square, making quite a spectacle for the local people who had gathered to gawp.

The teams were ready to roll!

CHAPTER 10

MEET THE TEAMS

The top attraction was the elephant.
Rosalba and Fandango were already
green in the face, clinging on for dear life
and suffering a kind of elephant-related
'seasickness' from the swaying motion of
the elderly creature as he plodded along.

Next in line was the Wilmington Ladies
Knitting Circle (there were five of these
respected ladies). They were … well, they
were knitting, non-stop, their needles

clicking endlessly as they worked on the woollen socks, jumpers, scarves and bobble hats that would keep them warm on the mighty Everest.

Then came the Watling Street Roman Re-enactment Society, perhaps the oddest-looking of the teams due to their insistence on maintaining the famous 'testudo' or 'tortoise' formation at all times. With their glorious red and gold shields interlocked above and in front of them, just like a tortoise shell, they looked like worthy competitors. If they got smashed by an avalanche, they would be fine!

The honey badger brothers were their normal, casual, sinister selves. They slouched around with arrogant calmness, little popcorn-eating squirrel Alfie their 'prisoner mascot' on display at all times in a wooden cage. To be honest, Alfie didn't seem to be too gutted by the situation! He spent most of his time shouting, 'Yay! More snacks! Alfie likes being a prisoner!' as the badgers fed him endless sugary treats of chocolate and toffee to keep him quiet.

Then, finally, there was Wilberforce. Yes, Wilberforce the high-altitude mole. Cold-hearted. Mysterious. International mole of mystery.

He just stood there with his massive rucksack on, looking as hard as nails.

'One team here will conquer the mightiest challenge of all,' Sir Archibald told the assembled teams: 'to cook popcorn on the summit of Everest itself!'

He nodded to two porters who staggered out with a wooden chest.

'In here is the one million pounds,'
Sir Archibald proclaimed.

He raised the lid, revealing the vast
riches within. The crowd gasped.

'It will go with us and be presented to
the winners on the summit. Now, let us
begin our epic journey … and may the
best team win!'

The wiggly line pulled out of the city
and headed for the hills. Inside the Pop-
O-Matic 3000 the squirrels gave each
other high fives. All they had to do was
wait for their chance to rescue Alfie!

What could possibly go wrong?

CHAPTER 11

THE EXPEDITION BEGINS

It was a sight to stir the soul. A grand and stately procession: the five teams out in front, and a wavering line of porters, cooks and camp followers tagging along behind.

The squirrels couldn't resist an occasional peek through the window of the popcorn machine, staring goggle-eyed at the Buddhist monasteries and exotic temples shrouded in the early morning mist. Cassie was enchanted by the rice paddy fields that flanked the way, the brightly clothed local families tending the green shoots, working side by side in the blazing sun.

Some children spotted the squirrels – a young boy and a girl who ran alongside the Pop-O-Matic, waving excitedly until they were chivvied away by Sir Archibald.

Higher and higher the expedition climbed, passing through tiny villages that clung like limpets to the ever-steeper mountain walls. The air began to get thinner, cooling rapidly as the steamy tropical valleys were left far below. The squirrels shivered in their little den, cosying up together to keep warm.

'When are we going to get some grub, pals?' Salty moaned, rubbing his tummy. They hadn't eaten for a while.

Night-time was when the squirrels suffered most. That was when the hunger hit hardest, when the cold was most extreme. The popcorn machine was a comfortable den, but until it was fired up and popping there was nothing to eat at all.

'Let's sneak into the nearest forest,' Ben said, 'and see if we can find some nuts or berries.'

The three squirrels waited until the

camp was quiet, then slipped quietly through the woods in the search for food.

The forest was an alien world. The trees were decked with creepers and vines. Things were slithering in the undergrowth. The night was alive with the chirruping and croaking of unseen insects. This was a tropical zone, very different from the neat and tidy British parkland the squirrels knew so well.

They found a tree loaded with spiky green fruits. 'Let's try these,' Cassie said quietly.

They had a chomp.

'Bitter!' Salty exclaimed.

'Too sour!' Ben added.

They tried a few more bushes. Nibbling at weird-shaped nuts. Chomping on berries that were sharp on the tongue. Nothing tasted right.

Tummies rumbling, the three friends went deeper into the rainforest.

Then they froze.

'Wh-wh-wh-what are those thingies, pals?' Salty stammered.

Eyes were staring at them from the shadows.

'Creatures,' Cassie whispered, 'hanging from that tree.'

The squirrels crept closer.

The eyes blinked fast.

'They've got wings!' Ben said.

'And teeth!' Salty gasped. Suddenly the night sky erupted. The tree seemed to explode. The squirrels ducked down as a thousand leathery wings brushed past them at high speed.

'Flying foxes!' Salty said.

The squirrels ran back to their hiding place. They felt sure that night would be a hungry one again.

But shortly before midnight ... *knock knock knock* – a gentle tapping on the glass of the Pop-O-Matic.

Two smiling faces, lit by moonlight. It was the two children who had run alongside them earlier.

'My name is Suresh,' said the boy.

'And I am Alina,' smiled the girl.

'We crept out to bring you some food!'

The thankful squirrels tucked into a rich meal – the children knew the forest fruits and had chosen tasty berries.

'It's good to know we've got some secret friends,' Cassie said as they curled up for sleep. 'We might need all the help we can get if we're going to rescue Alfie.'

CHAPTER 12

SINISTER STUFFINGS

The expedition had reached the high mountains.

The squirrels had been watching closely, looking for a chance to begin a rescue attempt to free their little friend. But the honey badgers kept their mascot under close guard, locked in his little wooden cage.

Shortly after sunrise the convoy arrived at a mountain village. It was home to a curious exhibition at the 'Life on Everest' museum.

That afternoon the teams went to see the exhibits. The squirrels also tagged along, making a secret journey to take a look through the window of the dusty old barn.

'That's spooky!' Cassie whispered.

In a dark corner of the barn they saw several stuffed animals.

A straggly bear, glass eyes staring eerily into nowhere. A stuffed snow leopard, the fur falling out, the tail half hanging off, one eye missing.

'Never mind "Life on Everest",' Ben said. 'More like "Death on Everest".'

'Those poor creatures,' Cassie said.

The squirrels ducked down as they heard the honey badgers inside, towing Alfie along in his cage. They were talking to the manager of the museum.

'These stuffed animals are very popular,' the man was saying. 'I pay good money for dead creatures to display.'

'Really?' Gritsky said. 'Even small ones?'

'Oh yes,' the man replied eagerly, 'especially if they've been to the summit of Everest. I'd pay a fortune for that! People would love it.'

'Interesting,' Fleabilly said. 'How would you like to go to the summit of Everest,

little Alfie?'

'Yay! Alfie to the top! Alfie loves it!' came the reply.

The honey badgers cackled between themselves.

Cassie turned to Salty and Ben. 'I wish I hadn't heard that,' she said, and nervously chewed on her lip.

'You don't think … ?' Ben found a lump filling his throat.

'Aye.' Salty shook his head. 'Bad news for wee Alfie, I reckon.'

'Even more reason to rescue him as soon as we can,' Ben added.

After lunch the teams rested back in their tents for a while. A cry from Sir Archibald broke the peace and quiet.

'Bring in the pack animals!'

A vast herd of bad-tempered, hairy, farting yaks was gathered in a nearby field. They looked a bit like bodybuilding shaggy cows but bigger; their horns were savage.

ROoooOAAAAAARGH!

A nearby yak raised its tail, scattering a generous portion of poo with reckless abandon.

Next to the honey badger compound, the friends heard the familiar sound of Alfie laughing.

'Yukky yaks! Poopy scoopy yakky dung!' he trilled.

The teams loaded all their gear on to the animals. Rosalba gave the leading yak a swift smack on the backside with a stick.

The beast lurched forward and the line followed on, the Pop-O-Matic 3000 buggy swaying from side to side on the rocky track.

'Next stop, Base Camp!' Ben whispered to the others. 'I reckon we'll get a chance to rescue Alfie there.'

Over the next two days the scenery changed. The expedition had reached the treeline – the zone where it is simply too high and cold for forests to survive.

Up here it was all about ice. Ice and snow. Rocky slopes. Jagged cliffs.

Cassie shivered as she looked out of the window of the Pop-O-Matic. Massive mountains were clustered on all sides.

'This is scary,' she said. 'A world without trees. A world without grass.'

'It's no place for a squirrel,' Ben added.

The trail steepened. Up to the heavens, twisting and turning as it went. The squirrels felt their tummies twist and turn as well as they saw the humungous drop beneath them, plunging chasms with raging whitewater rivers in the valleys below.

Sometimes the path crossed terrifying bamboo bridges. They swayed and rocked in the mountain wind, creaking worryingly as the caravan of yaks stomped across.

'Base Camp!' came a cry. The convoy came to a halt and the squirrels were able to sneak a peek at this most legendary of places.

CHAPTER 13

BASE CAMP BEAUTY

Cassie scraped ice crystals off the glass of their secret den, giving them all a perfect view.

'Wow!' she whispered.

It was certainly a spectacular and colourful scene: hundreds of igloo-shaped tents, a riot of greens and yellows, reds and blues.

'It's like a village,' Ben said.

'A fair few folk!' Salty whistled.

The three friends stared in wonder at the perfect circle of mighty peaks that surrounded the camping zone. Ice and snow was everywhere and the wind had a sharp, steely edge to it.

Quietly and carefully, they found an equipment tent to hide in, a perfectly

warm refuge from the wind.

At sunset, a noise began.

'Listen!' Cassie said.

Live music was coming from the largest
of the tents. Laughter and the sound of
dancing feet on the rocks could also be
heard.

'It must be a party,' Cassie said. 'Let's
take a look.'

The squirrels crept closer, scampering
from one boulder to another, keeping out
of view as they approached the huge tent.

'Nice music,' Ben whispered.

The rhythm was a stomping beat, driven
by violins, tom-toms and an accordion.
The squirrels found their hairy feet tapping
on the icy blue surface of the glacier.

Then they heard the unmistakeable
sound of Alfie.

'Yaaaaaay!' he squeaked. 'Wheeeee!'

They tiptoed around to the back wall of
the tent and were able to peer through a
flap in the canvas.

'Alfie!' Cassie gasped. 'Here he is!'

'It's him all right!' Ben exclaimed. 'But what on earth are they doing to him?'

In the centre of the tent the squirrels saw the most bizarre sight.

The honey badgers. Dancing. Throwing Alfie through the air between them as he chuckled with delight.

The entire tent was jigging about like crazy. Fleabilly had a violin tucked beneath his chin. He scraped at the instrument with jerky movements of his arm, his eyes wide and staring, his ears dripping with sweat.

His dance style was curious to say the least, somewhere between a Highland fling,

a solo tango and a Brazilian lambada.

Surrounding the badgers was a clapping crowd of climbers, loving every minute and taking pictures on their smartphones.

Alfie was part of the show, grinning wildly, whizzing through the air from badger to badger, like a circus performer flying from trapeze to trapeze.

'He's catching popcorn!' Ben whispered.

And so he was. Every few seconds, one of the spectators reached into a huge bag of popcorn and tossed a piece in the air. Simultaneously, Alfie would be launched, his mouth open wide for the treat, catching it skilfully on the fly and getting a roar of approval from the crowd.

'Whooopeee!' Alfie yelled. 'Alfie having the best time ever!'

Time and again he sped through the air as the music thudded away, from one side of

the tent to the other, all four limbs outstretched, fur rippling, eyes gleaming, snapping up a bit of popcorn on the way.

The game went on and on, and the other squirrels slipped away back on to the glacier.

'Och, it's freezing,' Salty said. He shivered as a gust of glacial wind came down from the mountains.

They retreated to the safety of their hideaway in the equipment tent, glad to curl up together, warming each other nicely.

'I don't like this at all,' Cassie said. 'Alfie's fun and games are all very well down here, but we all heard that conversation back at the Life on Everest museum.'

'It makes my blood run cold,' Ben said, 'the thought of little Alfie on show in that place for ever.'

'Glass eyes … ' Salty whispered.

The squirrels went deathly quiet as the chilling thought gripped them.

CHAPTER 14

MIND GAMES

Next morning the squirrels huddled together.

'Now, what ideas have we got for getting Alfie out of this mess?' Cassie said.

'We're so titchy,' Ben worried. 'What can itsy-bitsy squirrels do against big climbers and evil honey badgers?'

'That's why we need to use our heads, pal,' Salty said, tapping the side of his head with his paw.

'It's all about cunning,' Cassie nodded. 'The power of the mind.'

The three squirrels thought hard. A biting wind began to race across the ice outside the tent. They thought so hard their tiny brains began to ache.

Not a single idea came to mind.

Then Ben snapped his fingers.

'I've got it!' he exclaimed. He gestured to the large herd of yaks that was stationed nearby. They were penned into a type of enclosure surrounded by a drystone wall.

'What we need,' he added, with a cunning smile, 'is a *yak stampede*!'

'Cool!' Cassie said.

'What's the point of that?' Salty frowned.

'Come with me,' Ben said.

He led the way across the valley to the yak pen.

There were almost a hundred of them in total, a grumpy mass of hairy creatures chomping gloomily on the straw that the climbers gave them each afternoon, and poking each other with their horns when they got bored.

'All we've got to do is jump on to the wall and start yelling and shouting,' Ben said. 'The yaks will panic and burst through the gate and stampede through the camp!'

'I get it! The climbers will run for their lives,' Cassie said. 'And we can rescue Alfie in the confusion.'

'It's crazy … but it might just work!' Salty exclaimed.

The friends crept right up to the yak enclosure and waited until no humans were in sight.

Ben looked left, then right, then left again. 'Okay? Ready? Three, two, one, JUMP!'

The squirrels leapt on to the wall and began to scream. They jumped and pulled faces and turned somersaults and hollered until they were blue in the face.

Nothing.

Not a single yak paid even a *moment's* attention.

'We're too small,' Cassie sighed. 'We can squeak as loud as we like, but they couldn't care less.'

'Okay,' Ben said, a great smile spreading across his face, 'in that case we move on

to plan B.'

'Oh yes?' Cassie raised an eyebrow.

'Yes. We turn Salty into a *squak*!'

'A *squak*?!' Cassie exclaimed. 'It sounds scary … what on earth is a squak?'

'Now hang on a second, pals,' Salty said. 'I'm not sure I like the sound of—'

'I'm thinking about the secret of the Pop-O-Matic,' Ben continued, ignoring Salty, 'the way it gives us superpowers if we get zapped inside it.'

Cassie nodded. The memory of their last adventure was still fresh: a spin in the Pop-O-Matic that had turned them temporarily into giant zombie-like monsters.

'We heard Rosalba say she's going to fire off the Pop-O-Matic later this afternoon to make sure it's working,' Ben said. 'All we have to do is hide Salty and one of those baby yaks in there.'

Cassie's eyes widened. Salty gulped, his ears flat against his head.

'When he comes out, he'll be a giant

squirrel-yak!' Ben said triumphantly, his eyes shimmering.

'I get it!' Cassie said. 'All you have to do, Salty, is make a great **ROARRRR** and wave your arms around a bit. All the climbers will run away in terror, and then Ben and I can free Alfie!'

'Haaaaang on, pals,' Salty protested. 'How come it's ME that gets squakked?'

'Erm … because of your special forces skills,' Ben said, shooting Cassie a wink. 'Cassie and I wouldn't be tough enough to do it.'

'Aye, well,' Salty puffed up his chest, 'that's different, then.'

'It's a high-risk mission,' Cassie continued. 'It needs a specially trained military genius such as yourself, Salty.'

Salty licked his finger and smoothed down his eyebrows.

'Aye, there's not many have got the "right stuff" for the job,' he agreed.

'Plus you'll be truly terrifying as a

squak!' Cassie said.

'If that doesn't scare the living daylights out of these people, then nothing will!' Ben said.

'You're right,' nodded Salty. 'Plus, I'll wear my lucky battle kilt.'

'Er, battle kilt?' Cassie questioned.

Salty took a bizarre-looking yellow tartan outfit out of his little rucksack.

'Aye,' he said. 'McNutt tartan, from the glens. I wear it into all my battles, take it everywhere with me. It put the wind up those weasels at the battle of Weasel Ridge, I can tell you!'

Cassie sniffed the fabric.

'It stinks!' she coughed.

'Aye, well, it hasn't had much of a wash in recent times … but the smell is all part of the tactics.'

'Okay,' said Cassie, handing the kilt back with one paw holding her nose. 'Now you're all set. Good luck, Salty! We're depending on you!'

CHAPTER 15

YAKNAPPING

That afternoon the squirrels were on high alert.

There came some movement in the middle of the camp.

'Look! There's Rosalba. She's getting everyone ready for the popoff!' Cassie said. 'Looks like it's *squak* time.'

The squirrels went to the yak enclosure and lured a tiny baby yak away. They held straw in front of his little nose and he followed them across the glacier, nibbling at the treat and bleating happily.

The squirrels sneaked up to the Pop-O-Matic just before the crowd gathered. They grabbed hold of the unsuspecting baby and used all their strength to push him inside.

Salty got dressed into his special tartan outfit, making Ben and Cassie giggle as they saw the stretched, bulging kilt that barely covered their friend's ample frame.

'Do I look the business, pals?' Salty asked, swaggering back and forth.

'You look like a McNutt,' Ben said.

'You can do it, Salty!' Cassie encouraged. 'Remember, just scare them all away for long enough that we can rescue Alfie.'

Salty climbed with difficulty into the Pop-O-Matic and hunkered down in the bottom next to the bewildered baby yak.

Ben and Cassie scampered away behind a nearby rock as Rosalba and Sir Archibald approached, the other teams following on behind.

Curiously, given the freezing conditions, Rosalba wore a sequinned ballgown, and her face was plastered with even more make-up than normal.

Fandango arrived, carrying a huge sack of unexploded corn.

'You look ravishing, my dear!' Fandango told Rosalba, fixing her hand with a delicate kiss. 'Base Camp has never been blessed with such beauty.'

Ben and Cassie watched as more than a hundred climbers gathered around the

Pop-O-Matic. All the teams were present and a dozen journalists had appeared as well, covering the event for their newspapers. They fidgeted from foot to foot, cameras hung around their necks, shivering in the chilled air.

'Give us a few words, Rosalba!' Sir Archibald cried.

Rosalba was helped on to a rock so she could address the crowd.

'I was born a simple but very beautiful peasant girl,' she began, dabbing a tear away from her cheek. 'The other girls were happy to run barefoot in the turnip fields, eating raw vegetables morning, noon and night, but that was not my destiny! I knew I deserved the champagne lifestyle, and acting was the way I would achieve it! Yes, I was born to be an actress, my dear friends, my passion for the limelight drew me like a moth to a—'

'Get on with it!' came a shout from the crowd.

'Caviar and lobster, diamonds and pearls! I could have had it all if only those stupid directors had appreciated my *extraordinary* talent,' she continued, 'if only they had—'

'We want our POPCORN,' came another bored climber's cry.

Rosalba's mouth tightened into a thin crimson slit.

'Very well,' she said sourly, 'if it's popcorn you want, then it's popcorn you shall have!'

CHAPTER 16

BLAST OFF!

Rosalba slammed down the lever on the mighty machine. For a moment it merely hummed. Then a panel of red, green and orange lights zapped into life.

A ripple of applause broke out.

Rosalba frowned. She stepped towards the machine. 'But ... what's that?' she said.

She tapped against the glass where the tiny yak's face could just be seen through the kernels.

'There's a yak in there!' Rosalba screamed. 'We can't have this!'

Gears meshed together with a metallic clunk. The popcorn kernels began to glow.

Rosalba leapt like a gazelle on to the top of the machine, and frantically tried to prise open the lid.

'Rosalba! What on earth are you doing?'

Fandango stared in horror.

Steam spewed out of the guts of the Pop-O-Matic. A countdown rang out from a loudspeaker in the side of the machine.

'Ten – nine – eight – seven – six – five – '

The spectators stepped back, uncertainty in their eyes.

Rosalba grabbed the little yak and tossed him on to the ice.

The popcorn continued to shimmer. The glacier shook.

'Come away, my sweet!' Fandango cried. 'You can't be too near the machine when it … '

'There's something else in there!' Rosalba gasped.

She had spotted Salty.

'I don't believe it! It's that pesky fat squirrel!'

Ben and Cassie, watching every move, looked at each other with dread in their eyes.

'Four – '

She leaned over, reaching forward, trying to grab Salty. Salty squirmed out of reach.

'Oh no!' Cassie gasped. 'I have a bad feeling about this … '

Rosalba stretched further.

'Noooooooo!' yelled Fandango.

'Three – '

Rosalba tumbled into the machine.

The climbers gasped.

The lid of the Pop-O-Matic slammed shut behind her.

Some of the climbers rushed forward to try and help, but Fandango held them back.

'It's too dangerous!' he screeched. 'Stand back! Stand back for your lives!'

'Two – '

Everest itself seemed to vibrate. A mini-tornado of air began to spin above the machine like a sugar-saturated dust devil.

'Further back! Give it space!' Fandango panicked. 'We don't want any accidents!'

The climbers shuffled rapidly away.

'One – '

'Popoff!' Sir Archibald cried.

KERBAAAM!

The machine gave a final juddering shake. The popcorn kernels exploded all at once with a noise not unlike the final chord in the climax of a great symphony.

The climbers shivered.

Flashlights sparked off.

Popcorn squeezed out of gaps in the machine, shooting in every direction at high velocity.

The sound of the explosion echoed off the surrounding mountains, before gradually dying away.

For a few seconds all was silent.

The lid of the Pop-O-Matic flipped open.

The crowd gasped in horror.

Through the steam and popcorn haze a hideous monster was revealed.

'It's worse than we thought!' Cassie screamed. 'It's a Squirrel–Rosalba mix!'

'A SQUASHALBA!' Ben cried.

A ripple of disgust and terror passed through the crowd. Two of the

Wilmington Ladies Knitting Circle fainted. Even the Watling Street Roman Re-enactment Society broke their famous 'tortoise' formation and dropped their shields in shock.

'Alfie scared,' came a little voice from a cage. 'It's a two-headed yucky thingy as tall as the sky … '

'Gosh!' Sir Archibald exclaimed. 'That is the most horrific popcorn-induced mega-monster I ever saw in my life!'

Five metres tall it stood – as tall as a house. The body was covered with squirrel fur, but it had the shape of a human woman of a certain age.

The feet were remarkably hairy, bulging out of the supersized high-heeled shoes.

Salty's battle kilt was particularly awful, stretched like a miniskirt across thunderous thighs.

In truth it was a horrifying, stomach-churning vision dressed in yellow tartan from heads to toe.

Yes, you read correctly. *Heads*. I say 'heads' because astonishingly that was what the Squashalba had.

Two heads. Both gargantuan and fixed with an evil expression. One was Salty; Rosalba was the other. Exaggerated, enormous versions of both. And not in a good way.

Side by side they were: one body, two ugly great noggins, sprouting like huge rotting cauliflowers off the same stem.

And the strangest thing of all was that they hadn't even realised it …

Until now.

CHAPTER 17

FACE-OFF

Both heads turned, freezing in shock as they saw each other.

'*You*? You disgusting pesky squirrel! What are you doing … on … on *my* body?' Rosalba shrieked.

'*Your* body?' scoffed Salty, his mouth just inches from hers. 'This is *my* body, if I'm not mistaken.'

He brought up a hairy hand.

'That's squirrel fur,' he said triumphantly. 'Just look at the knuckles.'

'Okay, smarty-pants, what about the gold nail polish?' Rosalba pointed out.

Salty looked closely and grimaced. 'Yeuck! That's a bit girly for my taste!'

'And those are my shoes, if I'm not wrong,' Rosalba crowed.

Salty looked down, quivering. Then his expression lightened as he raised an arm.

'How about these biceps, eh?' he said triumphantly, flexing the elbow to pop the muscle.

'Pathetic!' Rosalba snorted.

'You know what the proof will be?' Salty said through gritted teeth.

'What?' Rosalba snapped.

'The tail,' Salty said.

The Rosalba head went pale.

'Th-th-th-there isn't … ' she stuttered. 'Surely you can't be … ?'

A great fluffy tail swept from behind.

'Noooo!' she cried.

'Ha!' the Salty head grinned extravagantly. 'See! That's 100 per cent squirrel, lass, and don't you forget it!'

'Well, I would agree with you if it wasn't for the ribbon and tinkly bells on the end of it,' came her reply.

Salty raised an arm to take the ribbon away, but Rosalba raised the other arm and blocked him.

'Get out of my space!' Rosalba glowered.

'My pleasure, lass, if you'd kindly get out of mine!'

'How dare you!'

'How dare *you*!'

Sir Archibald stepped forward. '*Ahem*.'

The Squashalba turned both of its hideous heads.

Two hundred rather terrified-looking people were standing there, armed with ice axes and tent poles.

'ATTACK!' Sir Archibald cried, and with that the mob rushed forward with a mighty cry.

The Squashalba spun on its high heels and zoomed away across the glacier at astonishing speed. Within minutes it had reached the lower slopes of one of Everest's neighbouring peaks. Higher and higher it raced, until it was out of sight amid the misty heights.

'Problem solved,' Sir Archibald said, rubbing his hands together with a satisfied sigh. 'That's the last we'll be seeing of *that* nasty creation!'

The crowd cheered.

'Alfie sad,' came a little voice. 'Alfie wants to play with the great big two-headed monster thingy.'

'Tomorrow we leave for the summit!' Sir Archibald announced. 'Then the *real* battle will begin!'

Over in their hiding place, Ben and Cassie shared a look of despair.

'First we lost Alfie,' said Cassie in shock, 'now Salty's gone. Whatever will we do?'

CHAPTER 18
FILLING UP

There was one consolation.

After the popoff there was plenty of popcorn around.

Ben and Cassie ate their fill that afternoon, their little tummies packed with the fluffy treat. Alfie was also fed very well by the honey badgers.

'We need to feed you up if we're taking you all the way to the summit,' they told the smallest squirrel.

'Yay! Alfie going to the top!' he exclaimed, dancing a little jig inside his wooden cage. 'Alfie's first mountain!'

'And your last,' muttered Gritsky, his eyes glittering.

All across Base Camp plans were being made. Teams were in their tents, talking strategy and writing lists, and the place was humming with excitement.

Cook popcorn. On the summit of Everest.

Eight thousand, eight hundred and forty-eight metres high. The tallest mountain in the world. A mountain that takes about ten weeks to climb, even if you are *not* planning to cook popcorn on the top!

'There's nothing for it now,' Ben told Cassie. 'We have to climb as well, keep trying to rescue Alfie.'

'I just keep thinking about those stuffed animals in that horrible place,' Cassie said, nervously playing with her tail fur.

Ben scratched his head. 'So what's the plan?' he asked. 'How do we climb Everest when we've never climbed before? There might be storms.'

'Avalanches,' added Cassie.

'Freezing cold,' shivered Ben.

'Frostbite.'

'Crevasses.'

'Then there's the things we need,' Cassie continued.

'Tents,' suggested Ben.

'Nice warm fluffy sleeping bags.'

'Food.'

Cassie sighed and put her paws over her face. 'Gosh, it's all so complicated. We'll *never* get it all organised in time. The teams are all about to leave.'

Just then they heard a voice, a child's voice.

'Hello?'

The squirrels peeped around the rock.

'There you are!' the voice continued. 'We've been looking for you everywhere.'

The squirrels blinked in surprise. It was the two children, Suresh and Alina. The same ones who had given them a midnight snack all those days ago!

'We were worried about you, so we brought you some things,' Alina said.

'Stuff that might be useful,' Suresh added.

They tipped open a bag and revealed the most wonderful sight. Cassie's eyes began

to well up as she saw the treasures within.
Squirrel-sized boots. Jackets. Ropes.
A little cooker. Special packets of
mountain food.

'It's everything we need; I can't believe
it!' Ben's voice was cracking up. 'Thank
you so much.'

The children gave the squirrels a hug.

'It's a pleasure,' Alina said. 'Good luck!'

And with that, the kindly children
started the trek back down the glacier to
the warmer lands of their home village.

Relieved, Cassie and Ben began to sort
through the equipment and food. It was
perfect for what they needed.

'Game on!' Cassie cried. 'We're coming
for you, Alfie. Nothing can stop us now!'

CHAPTER 19

BADGER BROTHERS

The teams pulled out of Base Camp at dawn, a long line of exotic adventurers with fame and fortune on their minds.

Sir Archibald was at the front, the chest containing the million pounds towed on a sledge by two porters behind him.

The other teams also had sledges sliding at the rear; it was the most effective way to get their popcorn-making machines to the top. All in all, it was the weirdest procession ever seen on Everest.

Ben and Cassie followed on, each step an adventure in its own right.

Straight away they were in the danger zone.

The Everest Icefall: a lethal obstacle of moving ice; a glacier that strikes terror into even the hardiest of mountaineers.

'It's like a maze,' Cassie said.

They gazed at the ice towers that soared on every side. Some were shaped like sails, others like pyramids, others like the fins of gigantic frozen sharks.

Then came the crevasses: huge splits in the ice.

'I can't even see the bottom of this one,' Ben exclaimed as he stood on the edge of one of the bigger cracks.

The depths were terrifying, the colour of the ice bleeding from white to kingfisher blue to inky black.

There was only one way to cross these hazards.

Ladders. Tied together, laid across the cracks like a bridge. Wobbly and sagging in the middle.

Each step was a tightrope act. The slightest slip would see them plunge into the frozen heart of the glacier.

Cassie found her legs wobbling as

vertigo – the fear of heights – struck her for the first time in her life. 'I hope they don't drop Alfie into one of these things,' she said, trembling.

This nerve-tingling zone went on for miles, the incline gradually steepening until the squirrels were puffed out and exhausted.

'The air's getting thinner,' Ben gasped.

Cassie coughed. 'I noticed!' she spluttered.

Each breath seemed to gather less oxygen than the breath before.

Finally the squirrels reached the end of the icefall. But their trial wasn't over; at the top of the slope they saw their arch-enemies, the honey badger brothers.

'Don't think we haven't seen you!' came a cry from above. 'You can give up any idea of rescue.'

Gritsky, the leader of the honey badgers, held up Alfie's cage. 'Your little friend is going to be the most famous squirrel in the world.'

'Yeah!' shouted Spudbasher. 'And we'll make a nice little packet out of selling him.'

Cassie felt her throat close up.

'Will they really do it?' she whispered. 'Sell him to that dreadful museum?'

'It's too awful to think about,' Ben shook his head.

'Yay!' yelled Alfie. 'Alfie loves it! Alfie famous for ever!'

'Stay strong, Alfie,' Ben called. 'We'll save you!'

The honey badgers turned to their popcorn machine. They started loading kernels into the top. Ben and Cassie watched, too exhausted to do anything other than sit, crashed out, on the ice.

'What are they doing?' Ben said. 'They're nowhere near the top.'

'I have a bad feeling about this,' Cassie said. 'They're putting too much corn in that machine.'

The honey badgers activated the switch.
Their popcorn machine began to hum.
Then it began to groan.
Then it *exploded*!

CHAPTER 20

POPALANCHE!

'Get down!' Cassie yelled.

The squirrels crouched low in the snow, covering their heads with their paws.

KERBUUUMBBAAAAABUMMMMBALUUUHGMA!

'Ha ha ha ha!' cackled Fleabilly. 'Our plan has worked a treat!'

The popcorn machine went off in an Everest-sized explosion of popcorn. The fluffy blizzard zoomed towards the heavens in a mushroom cloud that was so huge the sun was obscured and the mountain went dark.

Scientists later invented a new word for the phenomenon: a popalanche.

'That's a biggie!' Ben cried.

The popalanche raced down the slope.

Cassie screamed, 'Oh no!'
Ben yelled, 'Avalaaaaaanche!'
There was no time to run. Cassie and
Ben were swept away in the popcorn tide,

sent tumbling down the endless slopes in a flurry of arms, legs and tails, their feeble screams lost in the rumble of the mighty popalanche.

'That's the last we'll see of you, losers!' they heard one of the badgers yell.

'Watch out for the crevasse!' Ben screamed, spinning head over tail. Ahead of them gaped a fearsome split in the glacier.

The squirrels felt their tummies twist as they fell down the crack.

By the time they opened their eyes again they were sliding and slipping at thrilling speed down a great icy ramp.

It led into the depths of the mountain, and spat them out in a great tangled heap of fur into a huge icy cavern in the heart of the peak.

The squirrels blinked in astonishment. They were in a cave. A simply enormous space, the roof soaring up as high as a football stadium.

'The mountain is hollow,' Cassie said in wonder. 'Everest has got a hole in it.'

'Look,' Ben said, eyes squinting towards the shadows. 'I think there are things moving about in here.'

All of a sudden, a massive creature bounded out from the gloom. The squirrels shrieked.

The creature was two metres tall, and had great shaggy white fur, bright blue claws and glimmering bright blue fangs.

'Don't be frightened, little beasts!' the great yeti said. 'You are welcome to the Yeti Hotel!'

The squirrels untangled themselves and stood up shakily.

'Yeti Hotel?' Ben spluttered.

'This is where you live?' Cassie asked in disbelief.

More and more yetis were coming out of the shadows.

'Correct,' said the gigantic creature. 'Home to us yetis for 10,000 years!'

The squirrels gazed about them in wonder. The ice palace was packed. Yetis were everywhere. Big ones, little ones, young and old, hairy and bald.

'We thought you were endangered,' Ben said, baffled.

'Nearly extinct,' Cassie added.

'*Endangered? Extinct?*' The yetis roared with laughter at the thought of it.

'We're just very good at hiding,' the great yeti said. 'If humans don't see much of us about, that's because we don't want them to!'

A little yeti came to stand next to the big one.

'There's never been a better time to be a yeti,' the little one added proudly.

Cassie tiptoed to the middle of the cavern. She gazed into a bubbling grey pool of mysterious gloopy gunk.

'It's hot,' she said uncertainly. 'What is this?'

'It's a porridge geyser,' the great yeti said. 'A magic geyser. The only one in the world. Powered by geothermal forces deep within the planet.'

'It erupts every seventeen minutes,' the little yeti added. 'You can set your watch by it.'

'But where does the porridge come from?'

Ben stared bewildered into the gunk.

'The expeditions leave it behind,' the yeti said. 'They always bring too much and in the end they get sick of it and dump it in crevasses. We've been collecting it for almost a hundred years, adding to the porridge lake.'

At that very moment the ground began to rumble. A giant bubble of porridge rose in the middle of the lake. For a second or two it just sat there, a dome of oat slop forced to the surface by pressures from the heart of the earth.

CHAPTER 21

PORRIDGEY PAWS

The porridge geyser erupted. A great flubber-like fountain of porridge shot higher and higher, almost reaching the roof.

'Yay!' the yetis cried.

'Try some,' the biggest of the yetis offered. He scooped a massive pawful of porridge out of the bubbling lake and offered it, steaming and dripping off his fingers in sticky globules, to Cassie.

'It looks … lovely,' Cassie mumbled hesitantly. A grey blob dropped on to her foot with a splat.

'Go on, Cassie,' Ben teased, his eyes shining. 'Have a good old mouthful!'

Cassie poked out her tongue and took a lick. 'Mmmmm,' she said, her mouth strangely puckered up, 'how very, erm, delicious.'

Cassie flashed a look at Ben. 'Why don't YOU try some?' she said.

'Yes!' said the giant yeti. 'Why not?'

The giant yeti plunged a rather dirty-looking finger into the porridge lake and offered it up towards Ben's mouth.

Ben gulped. His tongue darted out, just the pink tip of it touching the gooey paste for a split second.

'Hmmmm,' he said. He wiped the back of his paw on his mouth.

'Yes, porridge is the business!' the great yeti said.

'There's nothing else like it!' the little yeti squeaked.

Ben reached into his rucksack, bringing out his emergency supply of popcorn.

He held out a fluffy piece.

'Forget about porridge. *This* is what you should be eating!'

The yetis leaned forward, sniffing the popcorn suspiciously.

'What is it?' the chief yeti asked.

'Popcorn!' Ben replied. He popped the piece in his mouth and chewed it.

'Popcorn?!' the yeti leader roared. 'Yetis don't eat *popcorn*!'

'No way!' the other yetis yelled in unison. 'It's bleeeeeurgh!'

'Well maybe we think porridge is bleeeeurgh!' Cassie replied. 'With all due respect.'

'It's not *porridge* that is bleeeeurgh!' the little yeti cried. 'It's *popcorn* that is bleeeeurgh!'

'Popcorn? It's the best food in the world!' Ben declared.

'*Porridge*,' growled the yeti.

'Popcorn!'

'Porridge!'

'Popcorn!'

'*Porridge*!'

'*Popcorn*!'

'**ROOOOOAAAAARGH!**'

Claw trembling, the giant yeti picked up a tiny piece of popcorn and raised it to his mouth.

'Papi, don't do it!' the tiny yeti called. 'Popcorn might be poisonous!'

'It is my duty, son,' he said, clenching his fangs and popping the snack in his mouth. 'For the good of the clan.'

He chewed the popcorn for a few seconds, his expression changing from one of disgust to one of cautious interest.

'Gosh!' he exclaimed. He grabbed a huge clawful of popcorn and stuffed it in his mouth. 'It's, erm, let me check a bit more … '

The others soon tried it. And, from that moment on, the yetis went crazy for popcorn. In less than five minutes all of Ben and Cassie's emergency popcorn supplies were finished.

'That wasn't half as bad as I expected,' the chief yeti said.

'We LOVES popcorn!' the little yeti added.

'All right, son, that's enough. Now it's time for some rest.' The chief yeti ruffled his son's fur.

The yetis got back to doing what yetis do best: lying on big hairy yak-fur rugs and yabbering away to their friends.

Wrapped up in their blankets, the two

squirrels found themselves snug and warm. Ben sighed as he felt his eyes closing.

'You know what? It's not so bad to be a yeti,' Cassie yawned.

'Apart from the porri … ' Ben fell asleep mid-sentence.

After the thrills and spills of the popalanche and the yetis' cavern, the squirrels were soon dreaming away nicely. Little did they know what the following day would bring.

CHAPTER 22

YETI RIDE!

Six a.m. The squirrels were already awake.

'Want some breakfast?' the little yeti asked.

SPLUNK! The porridge geyser flumped off, throwing yet more of the oat-based gruel into the air.

'Erm, thanks, but I'm not so hungry, actually,' Cassie replied.

They went to the entrance of the giant cavern, borrowing a pair of binoculars from the yetis to check out what was happening with the teams.

Through the goggles, Cassie saw a straggly line high on Everest. She picked out the Watling Street Roman Re-enactment Society, still tightly packed in their 'tortoise' formation, towing their medium-sized popcorn machine behind them.

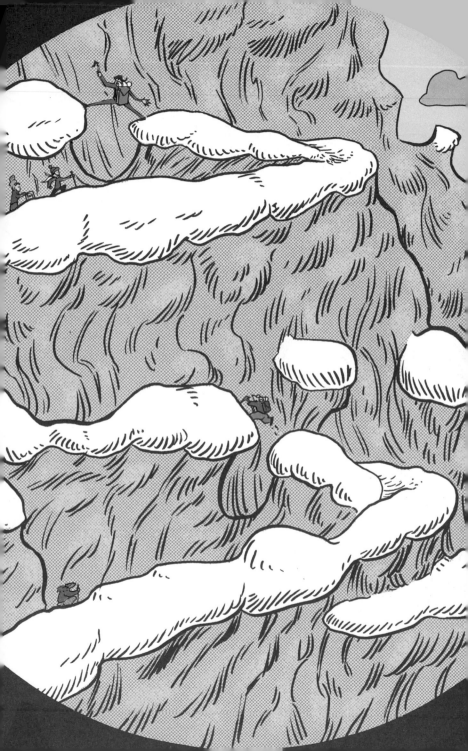

And there was Fandango, alone now that Rosalba had been morphed into Squashalba, single-handedly dragging the vast hulk of the Pop-O-Matic up the savage-looking slope.

The Wilmington Ladies came next, still knitting away even as they scaled the perilous heights. Each of these feisty ladies had an extra, giant knitting needle to use like an ice axe. From time to time they stabbed at the slope with incredible force.

Second from last was Wilberforce the high-altitude mole, still plodding away strongly. Finally came the honey badger brothers, Alfie in his wooden cage dragged behind on the smallest of the sledges.

'I can see Alfie!' Cassie said. 'But we'll never rescue him now. They're so high and we're too far behind.'

'It's true,' Ben sighed, staring at the floor. 'We've blown it.'

'Rubbish!' snorted the chief yeti. 'We'll help you catch up if you like.'

Ben and Cassie looked at each other, eyes gleaming.

'Get on!' the yeti said. 'We'll give you a piggyback.'

The squirrels literally jumped at the chance, leaping on to the biggest yetis' backs and grabbing hold of their long, soft fur.

'Whoaaaa!' Ben screamed as the creatures began to run. Cassie was hanging on for dear life.

It was a thrilling high-speed ride. Jumping crevasses. Leaping over rocky cliffs. Skipping across the stepping stones of tumbling whitewater streams with a hop, a skip and a jump.

The yetis were incredibly sure-footed. They never fell or lost their balance – even on the slippiest, shiniest ice they were fast and safe.

'Wowwwww!' Cassie cried, nose to the air. 'I love it!'

They crossed an entire valley in a matter

of minutes, then raced up a snowy slope on the side of Everest until they reached a huge gap in the ice.

It was the biggest crack the squirrels had seen on the mountain.

The galloping yetis got closer and closer to the void.

'I don't like the look of this,' Cassie cried, her voice wavering.

'Me neither!' Ben agreed through clenched teeth, his eyes watering with the icy wind.

The yetis didn't slow down one bit. In fact they sped up, leaping over the gaping hole in a single mighty bound which seemed to go on for ever.

It was a thrilling moment which left the squirrels breathless and whooping with excitement.

Then came the steepest section: an icy wall a thousand metres high. Ropes were dangling there, but the yetis ignored them.

'Look at their feet!' Cassie called to Ben.

He stared in astonishment. The bright blue claws on the yetis' feet were acting as grippy spikes, jabbing like daggers into the ice so they didn't slip.

Cassie looked down and gulped. Vertigo struck, a wave of dizziness at the enormous drop beneath them. Hundreds of metres down were the rocks and crevasses of the valley floor.

The slightest slip would mean certain death.

Cassie screwed her eyes shut. Raw fear gripped her. She grabbed ever tighter at the yeti's fur. She couldn't see but Ben was doing the same.

Kick. Smash. Pull. Jump. The yetis conquered in minutes what the teams had taken an entire day to complete. They gobbled up the distance like hungry caterpillars chomping on a leaf. Relentless. Unstoppable.

'This must be the camp!' the yeti said.

They came to flatter ground, a windswept

plateau. It was a bleak spot, with a hostile and threatening feel to it. Tents were dotted about, but the teams had hunkered down to rest after their climb.

Ben and Cassie shivered as they climbed down off the yetis.

'What a gloomy place!' Cassie exclaimed, taking in her new surroundings.

A savage blast of wind blew ice crystals into their faces.

'Mountaineers call this the South Col,' the chief yeti told them. 'We don't like to hang around here – there are always people about.'

'Okay, well, thank you so much for bringing us up,' Ben said gratefully.

The squirrels gave the yetis a big hug.

'A pleasure. Good luck with rescuing your friend,' the chief yeti cried.

The yetis turned, sat on their backsides and slid down the slope at a hundred miles an hour.

'It's sad to see them go,' Ben said. 'It seems even more lonely now.'

'Let's put up the tent,' Cassie said. 'Before the honey badgers spot us.'

They wrestled with the tent fabric and, after what seemed like an age, it was done. But it wasn't at all easy with the wind picking up.

It seemed that a storm was on the way.

CHAPTER 23

SUMMIT FEVER

'Summit day,' Ben called gently. 'Wakey wakey!'

Cassie poked her head out of the sleeping bag and yawned. Sleep had not come easily with the storm getting stronger through the night.

Her friend already had the little cooker lit. The delicious aroma of hot chocolate filled the tent.

They munched on some of the supplies that Suresh and Alina had brought them – healthy dried fruits and nourishing nuts.

From time to time the tent swayed and trembled as the wind beat against it.

As they enjoyed their breakfast, there came some noise from outside.

Crunch. Crunch. Crunch.

The sound of heavy footsteps on the ice.

The *click, click, clicking* of the Wilmington Ladies' knitting needles.

The Latin marching songs of the Watling Street Roman Re-enactment Society.

The swishing of the sledges being dragged along – one of which was carrying Alfie, others the popcorn machines, another the million pounds.

'The teams are going up,' Ben said. 'We'd better get ready.'

The two friends put on their mountain kit and stepped out into the blustery storm.

Cassie felt her whole body shiver as the cold bit into her.

'That's the coldest wind I've ever felt,' she gasped, watching her breath form miniature clouds.

Ben's teeth were chattering. 'Y-y-yes,' he agreed. 'We'd better move or we'll turn into b-b-blocks of ice.'

Ben and Cassie began to climb, following the footsteps the others had kicked into the frozen snow.

It was steep. But not as steep as the vertical tree trunks they often zoomed up and down back home.

They got into a good rhythm, taking twenty steps and then resting. Twenty steps then another little rest.

The air was thinner than ever. Thin enough that they truly struggled to breathe.

The wind was now much more than a blustery gale. It was becoming a terror. *Blast. Pause. Blast. Pause.* The sound of it whistling across the rocks was chilling. It became a howl, as if a pack of wolves was hunting up there in the blizzard. Time and again Ben and Cassie were blown off their little feet.

'Hang on!' Cassie encouraged her friend.

They clung on to rocks and scrappy bits of old rope. Anything to stop getting whipped away.

'My paws are going numb!' Ben admitted. 'I might get frostbite!'

Cassie put Ben's paws underneath her arms until they were nice and warm again.

They started to climb once again.

A few steps on, the squirrels noticed some imprints in the snow. Strangely shaped tracks.

'That's odd,' Cassie said, 'those almost look like high-heeled-shoe prints.'

Ben examined them, sniffing. 'Hmmm,' he said, 'you don't think … ?'

They stared up the slope.

'Better not to think about it,' Cassie said. 'The last thing we need is the Squashalba up here!'

They set out once more. Visibility was getting worse. It was like being inside a ping-pong ball. Upwards was white. Sideways was white. Downwards was white. The driving snow was even turning Ben and Cassie completely white.

'Someone's given up!' Cassie yelled, pointing.

Out of the blizzard came two groups, heading down the mountain.

'We've had enough,' the chief of the Watling Street Roman Re-enactment Society told the squirrels. They were all shivering violently and had even broken their 'tortoise' formation.

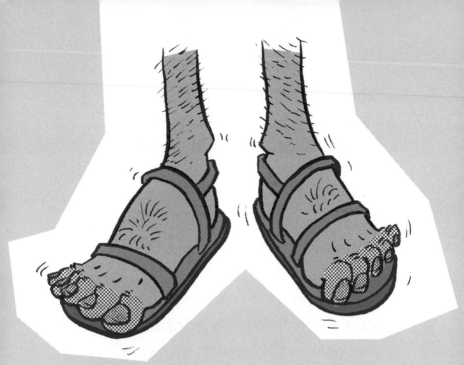

'We should have worn proper boots,'
one of the men said sadly. He pointed
to his open-toed leather Roman sandals.
His poor little tootsies were frozen solid.

'Have you seen our friend Alfie?' Cassie
asked. 'He's the one in the little wooden
cage.'

'Oh yeah, we saw him,' the chief
replied. 'Those honey badger creatures are
taking him all the way up to the top.'

'Was he sad?' Ben asked. 'Did he have
frozen tears on his tiny furry cheeks?'

The chief snorted. 'Are you kidding?' He's yelling things like, "Yay! Alfie having the best Everest expedition ever!"'

'Ah, hmmm.' Cassie wrinkled her forehead.

'Now then, we're going down to warm up and have a nice cup of tea,' the chief said. '*Vale*!'

Behind them came the Wilmington Ladies Knitting Circle, also retreating and looking most distraught.

'The worst has happened!' the leading lady wailed. She paused dramatically before adding, 'We've run out of wool!'

The ladies wished the squirrels good luck and hurried off down the slope. Ben and Cassie watched them go, quickly losing sight of them as the white-out of snow closed in.

'That's two teams down already,' Cassie said. 'And the hardest part is yet to come.'

They battled on, pushing hard against the bullying wind. The slope got steeper and steeper, the snow so deep that the two little squirrels sometimes sank in up to their noses.

The final ridge was the scariest place yet. Narrow. Crumbly. Slippery, too. The two friends had to concentrate on putting their feet in exactly the right spots.

'One false step,' Ben gasped, 'and … we'll … be … goners!'

CHAPTER 24

DEEP FREEZE

The ridge became thinner and thinner.

'The wind's getting stronger,' Ben panted. His words were whipped away instantly.

'What?' Cassie bent her head closer to him as he repeated the words.

'You're right,' she said. 'And the summit is still *miles* off.'

The two friends linked paws, giving each other support as they kept trekking ahead. The driving snow continued, pushing into their eyes and making them sting. Ice began to collect inside their tufty ears, so that from time to time they had to help each other break the icicles off.

'Even my nose is getting blocked up with ice!' Ben yelled.

He blew his nostrils hard, sending bullet-shaped plugs of ice bouncing off the ground with a sharp, pinging **SNAP!**

Cassie laughed as she dodged the snotty missiles. But then the smile on her face froze as she saw what was coming next.

The Hillary Step: a fearsome vertical cliff that the other teams had taken *ages* to climb. Getting the popcorn machines up it had been a fiendishly difficult task that had taken all their strength.

Now Cassie and Ben took on the same dangerous task.

Ben's heart leapt as he saw the plunging abyss on the other side of the face.

'How far down do you think that is?'

Cassie stared at the dizzying drop. 'The biggest fall in the world,' she whispered.

There was only one way to tackle the cliff. Cassie stood on Ben's shoulders and reached for a rope that was dangling there. It was *just* out of reach.

'Go for it!' Ben cried.

Cassie gritted her teeth, then jumped. She grabbed hold of the rope and pulled

herself up, puffing away like crazy. Then she carefully leaned back down and took Ben by the paw to help him get on to the rope.

It was an exhausting climb, taking nearly every bit of strength they had left. But, by working together, they had made it.

As they reached the top of the Hillary Step the summit came into view, like a fang of ice standing proudly above the clouds. The two friends flopped down on the ice, breath heaving, ready for a good rest.

'There it is!' Cassie puffed.

The summit of Everest: the ultimate quest in mountaineering.

The teams had almost made it. The honey badgers first. Sir Archibald and his porters second. Fandango third. Then Wilberforce the high-altitude mole bringing up the rear.

'They're on the final slope,' Ben muttered. 'It looks like the honey badgers are going to scoop the prize.'

'Let's just keep going,' Cassie said
blankly.

The squirrels continued along the ridge.

Alfie spotted them, blowing a kiss from
his little cage and waving excitedly until a
glare from Fleabilly made him stop.

Then an extraordinary thing happened.
Just as the honey badgers were about
to arrive at the summit, a huge creature
bounded up from the other side.

'The Squashalba!' Cassie cried.

The two-headed Squashalba raised
itself up and gave a ferocious battle cry.

Covered in ice from head to foot, the supercharged Salty–Rosalba monstrous mash-up megabeing looked even more fearsome than ever.

The honey badgers stopped in their frozen tracks. Even Alfie was struck dumb with surprise.

'Listen to us, pals, and listen good,' roared the Salty head.

The voice echoed spookily around the surrounding peaks as the Rosalba head continued.

'The Squashalba will be the one to activate a popcorn machine on the summit! None of you have got the courage to take us on! The prize will be ours and only ours! Ha ha!'

The Squashalba took a few giant steps towards the nearest popcorn machine, the one belonging to the badgers.

'Give me this!' The monster shook a massive fist.

But at that very moment, a great crash

of thunder shook the air.

The honey badgers scuttled backwards, scowling with shock as something most peculiar took place.

A single ray of sunlight punched through the cloud. It zapped vertically down, as tightly focussed and eye-tinglingly bright as a spotlight on a West End stage.

A tiny patch of the ridge was intensely lit.

And into that spotlight stepped the inscrutable figure of …

Wilberforce the high-altitude mole.

'I've had enough of this, old bean,' he said. 'Step aside, you two-headed twit!'

CHAPTER 25

HIGH
NOON

The wind died away. A deathly hush came over the scene. Ben and Cassie held their breath.

Wilberforce the high-altitude mole stared directly at the Squashalba, his eyes unblinking, his expression scarily blank.

Suddenly the silence was broken:

'Twitty! Twitty! Twit-twit!' Alfie sang from his little cage. 'Alfie loves it when the moley says twit!'

'Alfie!' Cassie hissed. 'It's not the moment to be saying silly things.'

'Okay,' Alfie said, clutching the bars of his little cage, his eyes shiny with remorse. 'Alfie never, ever, ever, say a silly thing ever again. Ever.'

The Salty head spoke first.

'Are you saying you're ready to have a go at the Squashalba, pal?'

Wilberforce nodded: 'Yep. I'll teach you a lesson you'll never forget, you tartan terror.'

'You'll take on the hero of Weasel Ridge? A measly little mole like you?' the Salty head scoffed.

'I certainly will,' Wilberforce confirmed. He slipped off his rucksack and cracked the knuckles on his overly huge paws.

'Come on then, pal.'

The mole did a pirouette. Lightning-fast. A huge leaping jump then took him high enough to poke the Salty head right on the nose.

The Squashalba roared, swiping at the mole and missing completely.

The mole gathered up snow. He had pressed a massive snowball together in a flash.

SPLAT! He hit the Salty head right in the eye.

'OW!' the Salty head roared. 'I'll squash you as flat as a moley pancake, you little rodent!'

The irate monster reached for the nearest item it could use as a weapon … the chest containing the one million pounds.

The Squashalba grabbed hold of the handles, raising the heavy container high above its two heads.

'Noooooooooooooo!' cried Sir Archibald in horror.

The Squashalba brought the chest crashing down with incredible force.

At the very last instant Wilberforce dodged to the side. The chest hit the icy ground with a resounding **CRASH!** Instantly it split open, the wood cracking into splinters as it disintegrated.

'Ah … ' Cassie looked around.

One million pounds in ten-pound notes whizzed into the air like confetti. For a split second they zoomed about as the

teams made desperate grabs for them. But a fresh, violent gust of wind rushed across the ridge.

A million pounds in cash blew away at 100 miles an hour down the icy slopes. The honey badgers ran after it, swiftly followed by the Squashalba, Fandango and Wilberforce.

Gone.

There was a stunned silence, then:

'Alfie's rich!' came a little voice. 'Alfie's the richest squirrel ever! Ten pounds! Yay!'

Ben and Cassie looked over to the little wooden cage where Alfie was staring, enchanted, at a ten-pound note he had managed to catch. It was the only note that had been saved.

That was when Sir Archibald dropped to his knees and began to cry.

CHAPTER 26

SUPER SLEDGE

'Now's our chance!' Cassie said. 'Let's get our Alfie free!'

They rushed to the little wooden cage and forced open the lock with an ice axe. Alfie jumped straight out and into their arms.

'Yay! Alfie happy!' The smallest squirrel of all gave his friends the biggest hug ever.

'Uh oh … ' said Ben, pointing down the slope. 'The honey badgers are coming back up and they don't look too pleased.'

Having failed to snatch a single ten-pound note from the greedy wind, Gritsky and his two sidekicks were storming back to the summit.

'That's our *prisoner*,' Gritsky growled from below. 'You put him back in that cage.'

'Never!' Cassie cried back.

'Then we'll capture you all,' Fleabilly said. 'Sell you ALL to the Life on Everest museum.'

'You'll be stuffed together! Goggled at by thousands every day,' Spudbasher cried crazily. 'The "Popcorn-Eating Squirrels of Everest!"'

'You'll be there for ever,' Gritsky added, 'or at least until your fur goes wonky and your glass eyes pop out.'

The honey badgers cackled as they powered up the slope.

The squirrels looked about them. There was nowhere to run to and the cliff behind them was almost vertical.

'We're trapped!' Ben said in alarm. 'What can we do?'

Cassie glanced at the sledge beside them – the one Alfie had been towed up on.

'There's only one way out of this.' Cassie's voice was serious. 'Are you thinking what I'm thinking?'

Ben smiled. 'I do believe I am,' he said.

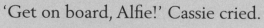

'Get on board, Alfie!' Cassie cried.

'Yay! Alfie go sledging!'

Alfie jumped on to the sledge. Ben and Cassie joined him a heartbeat later. The honey badgers were only a few seconds away, heading up strongly for the summit.

The squirrels pushed the sledge to the edge of the drop. Cassie gulped. Ben felt his chest tighten as his heart did a little loop-the-loop.

'Wow, it's pretty steep!' he said nervously. 'This could end in disaster ... '

The whole of Everest was below them. Eight thousand, eight hundred and forty-eight metres of ice fields and glaciers, ridges and crevasses.

'Alfie says go for it!' Alfie squeaked. 'Wheeeeee!'

'You're right,' Cassie exclaimed, 'we're the Popcorn-Eating Squirrels! Nothing stops us, ever!'

The three squirrels gave each other a squeeze.

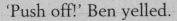

'Push off!' Ben yelled.

Cassie and Ben kicked the sledge off the edge, jumping on board as it started to slide.

The sledge accelerated. Faster and faster. The ice was super-slick, polished by the wind.

'Whooooo!' Alfie screamed. 'Awesome!'

'Ha ha!' Spudbasher snarled with pleasure as he saw the sledge whizzing towards him. 'I'll stop you, you pesky little—'

'To the right!' Cassie commanded.

Ben and Cassie put out their legs, steering the sledge.

The sledge veered sharply right. Spudbasher lunged. And missed.

'Dagnabbit!' he shouted.

Fleabilly grinned, his face contorted in an evil leer. He was next down the slope.

'I'll get 'em,' he said. 'Leave it to old Fleabilly if you want to get a job done right.'

Faster. Faster. The squirrels were hanging on for dear life.

'Head for the ramp!' came Cassie's instructions.

Just in front of the second badger was a small pinnacle of snow. Shaped by the wind, it looked like a snowboard halfpipe.

They hit it, dead on. The sledge flew upwards at breathtaking speed. Higher and higher, and over Fleabilly's head.

Fleabilly jumped, his outstretched claws just brushing the underside of the sledge.

'Drat!' he snarled.

Crash! The sledge touched back down. The squirrels held each other tight as the freezing air ran through their fur.

Last in line was the biggest of all the badgers. Gritsky.

The sledge whizzed faster than ever.

'Come to daddy,' Gritsky hissed. He clenched his fists and puffed out his chest. 'I've just about had enough of you stupid sq—'

Gritsky went flying upwards as the sledge bashed right into his legs before he could move. The squirrels held on for dear life as they tipped. For a couple of stomach-churning seconds it seemed they must surely be spilled out on to the slope.

'Weight to the left!' Cassie commanded.

All three squirrels leaned over, slamming the sledge back on to the ice as Gritsky crashed face down in a heap behind them.

'Wow!' Alfie yelled. 'Badger skittles!'

'Speedhogs!' Gritsky screeched, clutching his shins. He shook his fist at the rapidly disappearing squirrels. 'We'll get you next time, you'll see!'

'We're safe!' Cassie cried.

From there on it was pure excitement as the squirrels enjoyed the longest and fastest and most spectacular sledge ride in the world.

Alfie said 'Wheeeeeeeeeeee!' all the way down.

At the bottom of the mountain,

the yetis were waiting, steaming cups
of hot chocolate in their hairy fists. The
squirrels dragged their feet in the snow
to slow themselves to a stop.

'You haven't seen a two-headed giant
monster-type thingy, have you?' Cassie
asked them. 'We really need to get our
other friend back now.'

'Funny you should mention that,' the
chief yeti replied. 'Come with us.'

CHAPTER 27

FRIENDS REUNITED

The yetis took the squirrels down into
their cavern. In the middle was the
porridge pond, bubbling away nicely.

'That two-headed monster?' the chief
yeti said casually. 'It's in there.' He
pointed to the porridge pool.

'Yay!' Alfie cried. 'Alfie wants to go
swimming as well!'

'What?' Ben cried. 'How did that
happen?'

'We told you it's a magic porridge pond,'
the little yeti said. 'It can make any wish
come true!'

'We met your mutant friend earlier on,
and it came to us begging for help,' the
chief yeti said. 'It's a bit tired of having
two heads.'

'So we chucked it in the porridge,' the little yeti said, 'and told it to make a wish.'

The porridge welled up suddenly, a huge bubble rising and then popping with a puff of steam.

'Stand back!' warned the chief yeti.

The ground began to shake as the porridge bubbled. Then … **SPURT!** A massive plume of the gloopy Scottish oats erupted towards the ceiling of the cavern.

Two porridge-coated figures splatted on to the icy floor of the cavern.

'Salty!' Alfie cried. 'You're back to plumpy Salty gobby Saltiness!'

'Less of the gobby, pal,' Salty snapped as he shook off the gloop.

Salty and Rosalba shakily got to their feet. Porridge dripped from their ears, their elbows and their knees, as they checked they each now had their own bodies back.

'Thank heavens for that!' Rosalba exclaimed. 'I really couldn't have lasted

another second with that uneducated, boastful rodent wittering in my ear.'

'Boastful?' Salty crowed. 'The hero of the battle of Weasel Ridge doesn't need to boast, lass, believe you me!'

'That million pounds should have been mine,' she said, flicking Salty on the ear. 'It was you who picked the fight with that stupid mole … '

There came a snuffling noise behind them.

Slowly, they all turned.

Wilberforce the high-altitude mole was standing there.

'Did you say *stupid*?' he asked.

'Oh no,' Cassie sighed. 'Not *another* fight.'

Wilberforce sniffed.

'No, my dear fellows, it's all right. Say what you want. My scrapping days are over,' he announced. 'Something quite extraordinary has happened.'

He beckoned them all to come closer, pulling a tiny white object from his pocket.

A piece of popcorn.

'You see, even with the million pounds gone I decided I would still pop some corn on the summit,' Wilberforce told them. 'I mean, after all that effort it would have been criminal not to, yes? So I got out my little cooker and heated up some oil to pop a single kernel of corn.'

He showed them the popcorn. They all gathered in and examined it closely.

'Wow!' the chief yeti exclaimed. 'It's shaped exactly like a lotus flower.'

The others nodded.

'It's a sign,' Wilberforce said. 'The lotus is one of the eight symbols of the Buddhist religion.'

The yetis nodded wisely.

Wilberforce pulled the ruby-coloured robes of a Tibetan monk out of his rucksack and began to dress.

'I'm going to be a monk,' he declared. 'The Molai Lama. From now on it's mindfulness and mystic enchantment and all that stuff for me.'

'Yeah, that's right, pal,' Salty snapped. 'You're not hard enough to take on old Salty, the hero of the battle of Weasel Ridge, so you're running away to a *monastery.*'

Wilberforce laughed as he put on his rucksack. 'Peace to you all,' was all he said.

The puzzling mole strolled out of the cavern.

Rosalba wiped porridge from her eyes. 'Well, I'm trekking out of here and getting on the first aeroplane out of Kathmandu,' she hissed. 'And I hope I never clap eyes on any of you horrible vermin again!'

She fixed them all with an evil stare.

Alfie walked over and took Rosalba's hand. He stared at her adoringly, his big melty eyes all gooey and sweet.

'Will you be my mummy?' he asked.

Rosalba snatched her hand away.

'Oh, for goodness *sake*! Vile creature!'

Rosalba spun on her high heels and tottered off, porridge still dripping, towards Base Camp. A few moments later the squirrels and the yetis saw five exhausted-looking characters join her on the trek down the glacier.

Sir Archibald, Fandango and the honey badgers.

The honey badgers turned, giving a rude hand signal.

'You haven't heard the last from us,' Gritsky yelled. 'We'll get our revenge one day, you'll see!'

'Alfie loves you! Alfie says bye-bye,' Alfie called back, waving fondly. 'Alfie miss you already!'

'You know what?' Cassie smiled, tickling Alfie's ear. 'I think we need to get you home before you get us into any more trouble.'

'Will Alfie get popcorn at home?' Alfie asked.

Ben grinned. 'We'll see.'

The squirrels said their farewells to the yetis who had helped them so generously.

Later, back in the steamy valleys of the lowlands, they would find a way to thank Suresh and Alina, those helpful children who had also gone out of their way to be kind.

But for now it was time to start the trek.

The trek that would lead home.

The trek that would lead to new adventures.

The trek that would cause our four friends to link paws and cheer …

'POPCORN FOREVER!!!'

(Alfie: 'Yay!')

THE END

About the Author

Matt Dickinson is an award-winning writer and filmmaker with a passion for climbing and adventure. His proudest climbing achievement is standing on the summit of Mount Everest.

Matt is passionate about primary education, and tours primary schools across the UK and abroad. He talks about the inspiration for his books, reading aloud and nurturing a love of reading and adventure in even the most reluctant pupil. Engaging creative writing sessions can also be scheduled, and Matt will share pictures from his Everest expeditions – the inspiration for this book. If you would like a school visit from Matt please contact him: *www.mattdickinson.com*

Popcorn-Eating Squirrels Go Nuts on

Everest is the follow-up to *Popcorn-Eating Squirrels of the World Unite!*, where the squirrels first discovered their love of popcorn. They will return in a third adventure.

Matt also writes fiction for teenage readers, including the Everest Files, a popular trilogy set on the world's highest mountain.

Matt continues to climb and explore, and hopes to inspire the next generation of adventurers.